received
8-17-19

Table of Contents

Chapter 1

"I can see how this donut gets its name," Lilly said. "The Funfetti Donut is lots of fun!"

"Then it's a success. That's what I was going for," Heather said with a smile. She felt it was an especially sweet moment, both because she was able to spend some quality time with her daughter and because they covered in a thin layer of sugar. Finding the exact balance of color and donut-cake-base had been a deliciously dusty experience this time, but Lilly didn't seem to mind. She had a huge grin on her face.

"I bet we're going to raise a lot of money with these," Lilly said.

Heather nodded. She chuckled as she admitted that it was always her aim to make money with her treats when she sold them at her shop Donut Delights. However, profit wasn't the main reason for her business. She loved bringing joy into people's lives with something she had a talent for, even if it was just for snack time.

The Funfetti Donuts that she and Lilly were cooking up weren't for the display counter at Donut Delights, however. They were for a bake sale that Lilly's school was having. The PTA seemed to be banking on parents having time to help with the fundraiser in between school letting out and summer plans beginning. It did seem to work in Heather's case. She was happy to help with Lilly's school, especially when it came to bake sales. She would much rather whip up some of her world-class donuts for a cause than to sell raffle tickets or help with a car wash. However, her world had seemed very busy of late. It was sometimes hard to balance motherhood with owning a small business and, of course, solving the occasional murder.

Luckily, she and Lilly were able to team up and create a donut for the event together. Working together creatively as mother and daughter had been as satisfying as the confectionary concoction they came up with.

Lilly had suggested that they make something eye-catching and colorful so it would stand out on the bake sale table, and Heather had happily obliged. Using that idea as a springboard, Heather had come up with the cheerful Funfetti Donut. It was a basic vanilla flavor so it wouldn't scare away any potential buyers, and it had bursts of every color of the rainbow.

They were just about to bite into a sample of their hard work when they were joined by other hungry mouths. Heather's best friend and partner in solving murder cases, Amy, had come in to investigate the source of the delicious smell. She was joined by Heather's newest Donut Delights assistant Emily Potts.

"Are these the donuts for the bake sale?" Amy asked.

"Yes," Heather replied. "But there might be a few that can stay here for our enjoyment."

Lilly giggled as Amy and Emily Potts inched forward toward the colorful dessert. Amy picked up a donut right away to begin her edible enjoyment. Emily Potts was more reserved. She was Heather's most studious assistant and carried a notebook around with her to take notes on the new flavors. True to form, she opened her notebook to a blank page and prepared herself to write about the newest donut.

"What is this colorful one called?" Emily asked.

"This is the Funfetti Donut," Heather said. "It was Lilly's idea to make something so colorful to attract attention at the sale."

Lilly beamed and then helped Emily Potts with her notes, making sure she spelled "Funfetti" correctly. To make the note page match the fun theme, Emily Potts allowed her to doodle some happy donut drawings in the margins.

"I think it will work," Amy said. "I can't take my eyes off them. Or at least I can't until they've all been devoured, which I think I'm about to embark on."

Heather jokingly hit Amy's grabbing hands away from the table, but did say seriously, "We can't eat them all. They're for Lilly's school."

"But school's out for the summer," Amy pleaded.

Heather allowed her friend to have a second helping, but then started boxing up the other donuts to hide temptation.

"They're raising money for new playground equipment," Heather said. "I think the hope is that they will raise enough with this event that they can start ordering and building soon. Ideally, the new playground would be ready when school opens in the fall."

Heather was being very efficient with boxing up the donuts and had almost put them all away before she realized that Emily Potts had never had her sample. She handed one to her grateful assistant.

"It's delicious," said Emily. "Sweet and simple, but beautiful to look at."

"It's a vanilla cake base with Funfetti sprinkles inside to give it a colorful look. Then it has vanilla icing on top with even more sprinkles."

"It's like a cake and a donut at the same time," Amy said. "I love when you combine my favorite desserts together. Whether it's cake and donuts. Or pie and donuts. Or cinnamon rolls and donuts. Basically, anything and donuts."

Emily Potts finished her donut and notes with a smile. "I'm sure everyone at Donut Delights will love these as much as we do."

"I hope so," Heather said. "But these guys are headed to the bake sale first. Then I'll display them here."

"Do you need any help bringing them over to the sale?" Emily Potts asked, always willing to assist.

"Amy is going to help me," Heather said. "If I can still trust her around the donuts."

"Don't worry," said Amy. "If I eat any of the donuts at the bake sale, I'll pay for them and donate to the cause. I bet they could get a new swing set with all the donuts I eat."

They all laughed. Then Heather got down to business making sure that Emily Potts and the other assistants could run the business while she was out. Amy and Lilly helped Heather bring the boxes of Funfetti Donuts to her car.

"Thanks for doing this, Mom," Lilly said.

"I'm happy to," Heather said. "And let's hope our Funfetti will lead to fun on a new playground!"

Chapter 2

"Here you go," Heather said, handing Funfetti Donuts over to a mother and son who were patrons at the bake sale. It was hard to tell who was more excited about trying the fun flavor because they both had big grins and expectant eyes. They took appreciative bites and walked off together in good spirits.

Heather and Amy were selling their donuts at a table and enjoying the atmosphere. The sale had only wanted parent volunteers, so they had dropped Lilly off with her dad who was planning a trip to the movies for the two of them. Ryan had kissed

Heather and told her how happy he was to have an afternoon off from investigating murders. The detective had made sure to knock on wood after that comment, and Heather and Amy had left him on his own to see if the superstitious behavior would hold up.

The bake sale was set up under a veranda in one of Hillside's parks. The location's original intention was to allow for bands to play for residents who could either wander around in the park's natural beauty while listening to music or to set up lawn chairs and enjoy a concert. School marching bands and an occasional garage band did play songs there, but the veranda was used just as often for other fundraising activities.

Heather had been concerned about all the sweet goods being out in the Texas heat for the bake sale, but the weather was being mercifully kind and wasn't baking them and the desserts in its sun. As she looked around, she saw that other members of the PTA had planned ahead and had coolers for the items that should stay chilled and for beverages. She was also proud to see that her donuts were one of the fastest selling items on the tables. Either the knowledge that they were from the Donut Delights baker or Lilly's idea about bright colors (or a combination of the two) were causing her Funfetti Donuts to be quite a success. This was not lost on Amy.

"Your donuts are really flying off the shelves. Or table, rather."

"I know," Heather said. "And if I see who I think I see coming, they're about to disappear even faster."

Heather smiled as her suspicions were confirmed. Her favorite customers at Donut Delights and now her close friends, Eva and Leila, were approaching the table. The two older ladies looked ready to buy a good amount of the bake sale and carry it away with them. They were carrying a huge tote bag between them.

Heather knew how much the two ladies loved their sweets, but she was a tad concerned about how much they might end up bringing home with them. This was mainly because they were still staying with her until their house was repaired after it was a victim of arson. Her kitchen cabinets were already bursting with sweet treats, and she wasn't sure how much more they could hold.

"I don't know how I feel about this." Eva joked, "You're hiding a new flavor from us."

"After all our loyal years of patronage at Donut Delights, you'd hide this colorful fellow from us?" Leila asked with mock sorrow and indignation.

"I'm not hiding anything," Heather laughed.

"You did find us pretty easily," Amy added.

"These donuts will be at Donut Delights soon, and I'm sure some will appear in my kitchen tonight so that you won't be missing out on any donuts."

Eva and Leila looked at each other.

"I'm not sure we can wait that long," Eva said.

"No new donuts until tonight?" Leila wailed.

"That won't do. We'll have to buy some now," Eva said with a wink.

Heather prepared the donuts for her friends, and they happily took a bite.

"I know I say this about all your donuts, but this is delicious," Leila said.

"And we're very happy to support the school," Eva said. "Especially if we get something tasty in return."

"Speaking of getting tasty things, I can't help but notice the giant bag you two brought to the bake sale," Heather said.

"We're professional investigators, and I have a suspicious mind now," Amy said. "You're not trying to get rid of a body in that thing, are you?"

The two older ladies laughed.

"No, no. Nothing like that," Eva said. "This is just for snacks."

Heather's eyes widened, but Eva and Leila quickly reassured her.

"It's not all for us, dear," Eva said.

"Even I couldn't eat that much," Leila said.

"We're going to check on the crew that is repairing our house and bring them some refreshments in exchange for their hard work," Eva explained.

"Taryn Turner said that we could stop by anytime," Leila said.

"Though we might have to wear a hard hat if they're working on the wall structural damage."

"Luckily this outfit goes with anything," Leila joked. "Even hard hats."

Heather laughed. She was glad that the repairs were going well. They had first met their home renovator when she was under suspicion of murder, but since she had been cleared of wrongdoing, she had proven herself as a capable and enthusiastic home design and repair expert.

It looked as if the renovations might be done soon and Eva and Leila would be able to return home. Heather had mixed feelings. She knew the ladies loved their home and would be happy to return to it. Heather wanted them to be as comfortable as possible, but she had to admit she would miss them when they moved out of her living room. It had felt like she had two grandmothers that were living with her. She loved both Eva and Leila in their own right, but because she missed her own dearly departed grandmother it was nice to have matriarchal figures at home.

Then again, she knew that these friends would never be far from her life. Regardless of where they lived, they all felt like a family, and they would stay close, especially if Heather kept cooking up new donuts for them to try.

Eva and Leila bought some more Funfetti Donuts, both for themselves and for the crew.

Then they went to browse the other options at the bake sale and walked away talking about their preference between blondies and brownies.

"With so few donuts left for sale, I won't feel too bad when I run away from you," Amy said.

"It's almost that time?" Heather asked.

Amy nodded. Heather had been grateful that her bestie accompanied her today, both because she loved spending time with her and because it meant she had an ally at the event. Heather felt like she wasn't great making small talk with the other parents, especially with the President Marcia Lindau and her cronies. They seemed to make everything into a competition. Heather knew that emotionally she would always think Lilly was the best child in the world. When it came to markers that could be compared objectively, well, Heather didn't really care who jumped the furthest or scored the highest. She wanted Lilly to do the best that she could do, and strive to accomplish her own goals. Heather also didn't like to wave her child's accomplishments around like some sort of flag.

Heather liked to talk about Lilly when people really cared about hearing how she was doing, or when another parent wanted to talk and relate to how tricky parenting could be. However, she didn't like to try and "one up" the other parents, and that seemed to be the main hobby of Marcia Lindau and friends.

Amy had told her that she couldn't stay the whole day though. She and her boyfriend Jamie had just selected the house they were going to rent together. They had plans to go out to dinner and then start making the tough decisions about furniture.

"I'm not sure which couch is going to win out," Amy said. "I think mine will match the new space better, but his is more comfortable."

"Maybe you could put a slipcover over his?" Heather suggested.

"Maybe," Amy agreed.

Heather's thoughts turned to the unpleasant task ahead of helping her friend move. It would probably feel like double the work because items would be coming from both her and Jamie's former homes. However, she didn't want Amy to think she wasn't excited about the move and pushed the heavy lifting thoughts away before she grimaced.

Amy left, and Heather sold her last few donuts. She wondered if she should have brought more supplies, but decided she had already brought in more than some of the other volunteer bakers.

She also realized that she shouldn't just leave after all her goods were sold. She should probably check in with some of the other PTA members and see if there was anything else she should do. She took a deep breath and went to face the music.

Chapter 3

"It looks like the bake sale is going well," Heather said as she joined Marcia and a few other young moms by the pie table. Marcia looked impeccably made up and was wearing a stylish cardigan that matched her slacks and her painted nails. She was wearing heels that Heather thought were rather impractical for a bake sale in a park.

"I'd agree and say it has been very successful," Marcia said. "Our hard work has paid off, and I believe we'll be able to get the new playground equipment. The children will be provided for."

The three moms who she had been talking applauded at this mini speech. Heather wasn't quite sure why and refrained from clapping herself.

"I don't mean to brag," Marcia continued. "But my blackberry pies have been quite a hit. I've nearly sold out."

"That's wonderful," Heather said. "Is there anything else I should help out with here today?"

"No, no," Marcia said. "Just sell your baked goods, and that's it. We'll be here until sundown. Then I have the Parks Department coming to help clear up the tables. Hopefully, most of our desserts will be sold by then."

"Well, I've already sold out of mine," Heather said.

"What?" Marcia asked. "What did you bring?"

"Donuts," said her friend with curly hair.

"Oh, well those snacks are rather small. And I bet you didn't bring too many."

"She did bring a lot," the curly haired friend continued. "She's the lady from the donut shop."

"Quiet, Claire," Marcia said to her. Claire didn't seem upset by the comment but rather resigned to the treatment.

Marcia turned to Heather. "So, we have a professional here?"

"I guess so," Heather said. "I am the owner, head baker, and flavor creator at Donut Delights."

"That's fantastic. It's so nice to have a real baker here," Marcia said.

"I'm really only good with donuts," Heather confessed.

"It's still really great to have a professional be part of our events." Heather almost believed the compliment from Marcia until she continued with, "Of course, I'm sure donuts are less expensive than pies. That might be part of why they sold so quickly. Food for the poor masses."

"Sure," Heather said.

She had wanted to avoid getting into a competition about their children, and now it seemed that they were competing themselves. Heather didn't care about winning. She just wanted to know if she could leave early after selling all her donuts without causing waves.

"Because my pies are rather expensive. They are high end. But they're still selling rather well."

"That's great," Heather said again. Her patience at playing nice with this rude woman was wearing thin. However, she wanted to keep things on good terms for Lilly and the school's sake.

It was apparently very important to Marcia that she have the most successful dish at the bake sale. Heather knew that she was very talented when it came to making donuts, and she probably did create the best treat there that day, but having the title of "best baker at bake sale" wasn't important to her. She just wanted the patrons to enjoy some snacks and donate to a worthy cause. Wasn't that what this was supposed to be about? Wasn't this about helping the school?

"Well," Heather said. "If you don't need me, I'm going to head out."

"Well, that's very interesting," Marcia said.

"What is?"

"Your leaving early."

"You just said you only need me to sell my own snacks, and that other people are cleaning up the tables. I sold my snacks, so I thought I was done," Heather said.

"You can be done if you want to," Marcia said. "I just thought it was interesting that we haven't seen you at many of the PTA meetings. Why is that?"

Heather's real answer was that she didn't like the president of the organization, but she knew she couldn't say that to Marcia's face, so she opted for a casual, "I've been busy lately, but I'll try to come to more."

"That's true," Marcia said. "You must be really busy what with running that little muffin shop of yours."

"Donut shop," Claire said.

"Quiet, Claire," Marcia responded. "It must be difficult to balance raising a child with running a business. What was your name again?"

"Heather Shepherd."

"Why does that name sound familiar?" Marcia asked.

"Because she's in the paper a lot looking at dead bodies and chasing murderers," Claire said.

"How gruesome," said Marcia.

"I think of it as helping to see that justice is served," Heather said. She had already stifled a groan. She had never been a huge fan of the Hillside Reporter's write ups on her casework, and the fact that it was giving fodder for these gossipy moms was making her even less enthused about it.

"It must be hard to balance all those things," Marcia said in a soothing voice.

"It can be," Heather said.
"I just hope that your little Lilly doesn't get the short end of the stick."

"Lilly is just fine," Heather said. "She has two parents that love and care for her."

"We don't see much of her at afterschool activities. We see less of you at PTA meetings. But we still don't see a lot of her either."

Heather shook her head. She shouldn't have to explain her family to these women. Lilly took part in the activities she wanted to take part in, and at the moment she wasn't very excited about the sports programs that had been offered. That didn't mean that Lilly didn't have a rich and fulfilling life outside of school. Lilly liked to volunteer at the local children's shelter because she used to live there, she liked taking care of the furry family pets, and she liked writing stories about dinosaur detectives on her pink typewriter.

"Lilly takes part in the activities she likes. She has lots of friends and takes part in things outside of school."

"I hope that's true and that you're not just telling us this," Marcia said.

"I really have to get going," Heather said. "I'll see you at the next bake sale."

"I hope so," Marcia said. "I hope you're not just doing the bare minimum with us."

"The bare minimum is no good for the children," Claire said. "What if everybody decided to do that?"

"Then again," Marcia said. "Maybe you feel like you can get away with it because Lilly isn't your real daughter."

"What?" Heather asked, hoping she had heard her wrong.

"Maybe you feel like you don't have to do as much for the school because Lilly's adopted. She's not your real daughter."

"Lilly is my daughter," Heather said and decisively marched away.

She felt she now understood where the phrase "seeing red" came from. When she heard those words come out of Marcia's mouth, she felt like her whole vision had glossed over a crimson color.

Chapter 4

Heather was still furious when she reached the end of the bake sale area and realized she might be too angry to drive. She didn't want her emotions to cloud her judgment on the road, and so she stopped at the last table at the bake sale and pretended to be selecting a scone.

"Is everything all right?" A voice asked.

Heather realized she had been taking several deep calming breaths that probably looked excessive for the decision of choosing a bake sale item. She looked up at the woman being the table. She had a kind face and a messy blonde ponytail.

"I'm fine," Heather said. "Just trying to choose one of these."

"I'm going to be honest with you," the woman said. "They're all store bought."

Heather laughed at the wry way she told her and felt some much-needed relief of tension.

"If you want to make a donation to the school by buying one, go right ahead. But if you want something home cooked and savory, maybe try another table. I'm no chef."

"I can only make donuts," Heather said. "Most other things I make are a disaster."

"I'm Lisa Luft," the woman said with a smile and an outstretched hand.

"Heather Shepherd," she responded, shaking hands.

"I know that name. You're a mom here, right?" Lisa thought about it. "Lilly?"

"Yes!"

"Such a sweet kid. I'm Renee's mom."

Heather placed the face and nodded. "I can see the family resemblance."

"We're both very blonde. But she always has scraped knees. I don't know where she inherited her sense of balance because her father and I don't walk into walls."

Heather instantly felt more at ease and had to remind herself that not all the parents at the school were as cruel as Marcia Lindau.

"How is your selling doing?" Lisa asked.

"I actually sold all my donuts. I was going to head home," Heather said.

"That's awesome," Lisa said. "I keep scaring my customers away with my honesty. But as long as they give money to one of us, then the playground is supported."

"It's so refreshing to hear you say that," Heather said.

"Oh. Were you spending time with the Marcia crowd?"

Heather nodded.

"Then I can understand why you were upset before. It's not my scones. It's those ladies," Lisa said. "I'm not a fan of them either. That's why I have my set up over here, far away from their clique."

"I don't know how they can have someone who makes nasty comments in charge of the organization," said Heather.

"I think she does raise a lot of money. So, we adults suffer from having to deal with her, but the kids profit in the end with what she raises."

Heather nodded.

"What did she say to you? Do you want to talk about it?" Lisa asked.

"She said Lilly wasn't my real daughter because she was adopted."

"Well, that's ridiculous," Lisa said.

"Thank you. I knew it was, but it was still upsetting to hear that some people think that way."

"Well, I'm sure the courts and your family disagree with her."

"It's not just that. She didn't seem to remember much about me," Heather said. "The only thing that she remembered was that Lilly was adopted. And that shouldn't matter."

"She might remember more than she lets on. She just likes to make people feel bad. But what Marcia Lindau thinks doesn't bother me," Lisa said. "And I'm definitely not going to her wine parties anytime soon."

"What's that?"

"Oh, I hope you're not heartbroken if you weren't invited," Lisa said. "Apparently, some PTA moms get together with her and drink wine. Could you imagine that? Choosing to hang out with her for fun?"

"No, I can't," Heather said. "Thank you for cheering me up. I think I should get home now."

"Have a good night."

"Good luck with your scones."

"They'll need it."

Chapter 5

Heather was curled up on the couch with the other man in her life besides her husband, her doggy best friend, Dave. Dave loved donuts and cuddles and was settling for the latter. She hugged her canine friend and had trouble determining whether he was actually losing any weight or if he had been cheating on his diet and someone was sneaking him donuts.

It was a rare moment for just Heather and Dave to be alone. She scratched behind his ears, and he licked her face to show his appreciation. She pushed him down but smiled. She didn't need doggy breath to let her know he loved him. She did appreciate the hugs though. She didn't want to admit it, but Marcia Lindau's words had rattled her. It wasn't that she said Lilly wasn't her daughter. That was easy to dismiss as untrue. However, when she spoke about Heather balancing her work-life and crime solving with being a mother, it made her second guess if she really was giving Lilly enough time.

Lilly had a fun time with her dad at the movies, though they both joked about how there should be donuts for snacks instead of popcorn. They had a nice family dinner together, and Heather had put Lilly to bed that night. She told her a bedtime story that night. Lilly thought that hearing more stories might help her with her own writing and asked to hear one, excited to hear what her mom would offer a tale of. Heather's story ended up being a mixture of a fairy tale and an old case that she had solved. She removed the murder from the tale because it was right before bed, but kept the searching for clues, and in the end, everyone lived happily ever after. Lilly seemed to enjoy it but fell asleep soon after. Heather decided that her falling asleep was the point of the story, rather than an insult saying she was boring.

Their kitten Cupcake had fallen asleep as well and was sleeping next to Lilly. The more Heather pet Dave's tummy, the more Zen-like he became, and it was possible he would fall asleep too. Heather was trying to push her thoughts away from Marcia Lindau when she heard movement at the door.

Her husband Ryan had returned with Eva and Leila. It had been a late night for the two ladies who attended a Pickleball Tournament, and Ryan had agreed to chauffeur so they wouldn't have to drive at night. Heather had not known what Pickleball was but discovered it was a cross between badminton and tennis, and was a sport that all age levels could play. Eva and Leila had known some people from Hillside Manor that were playing and had decided to go cheer them on. However, as they described the game, it seemed that as the rounds went on, they had joined in playing. The ladies were excited about their adventure, but as the adrenaline wore off, it became clear that they were exhausted.

"Come on, Dave," Heather said. "Let's go into the kitchen so these ladies can rest up after their victory."

"To be honest, I'm not sure if we were keeping score at the end,"

Eva said. "But it was a grand time."

"I wouldn't have thought that a game with such a silly name would be as fun as it was," Leila said.

Heather wished them goodnight but had trouble moving Dave. "All right. You win," she said. "Come with me to the kitchen and get a donut."

With that inducement, Dave raced off the couch and followed her into the other room.
"Can I get a donut too?" Ryan joked, following her.

"A donut and a kiss," Heather said, and she fulfilled both of those requests.

They sat down to enjoy a late-night snack together while sharing some bits with a tail-wagging Dave.

"I only caught the very end of the game," Ryan said. "But it was fun to see them play. Leila is fast, and Eva has good aim."

"If they play again, I'd like to watch them play."

"It looked like everyone was having a blast," Ryan said. "But not you. What's wrong?"

Heather told him about how the comments from the bake sale were on her mind.

"Do you think my time is split too many ways?"

"I think you're a wonderful mother. Lilly knows that love her and that you would drop everything at a moment's notice for her if she needed you," Ryan said. "If you were in her hair all the time, it would drive a kid crazy."

"So, you think I'm not here all the time?"

"I think it's like one of your recipes. You need to have the right balance to keep everything together and tasting good. Sugar is important, but if you were all sugar, it wouldn't be a donut. And too much milk would make you too watery. Do you know what I mean?"

"I think I know what you mean. And thanks," Heather said. "But based on that metaphor, I'm not letting you into my donut kitchen anytime soon."

Ryan chuckled and gave her a hug. It was short-lived, however, because he was interrupted by his cell phone ringing.

"Shepherd," he said, answering it. Based on the responses he gave, Heather got the impression that he was being called to a crime scene. Her suspicion was soon confirmed.

"Looks like my day off is leading to a night of working."

"There's been a murder?"

Ryan nodded. "Looks like poisoning. An ambulance tried to save the woman but was too late. It's been declared a murder already. I should get over there. Do you want to come and investigate?"

"Sure. I'll call Amy, and we can help you. Where are we going?"

Ryan showed her the address
that he had written down and
said, "Lindau residence."

"Uh oh," Heather said. "I want to
help with this case, but I think you
need to officially determine that
I'm not a suspect first."

Chapter 6

Heather was waiting for Ryan outside of the Lindau house, and she felt she had been waiting a rather long time. She had already counted all the flowers in the yard and didn't feel up to the task of counting the stars up above.

Luckily, Amy soon joined her to relieve her boredom.

"Are they really considering you a suspect?" Amy asked. "You need to stop fighting with people who end up as murder victims."

"Firstly, I didn't fight with her. She made some mean comments, and I left. Secondly, I offered up this information freely so Ryan could clear me and we could still help solve the case. I barely knew Marcia before today, and I didn't have a motive to be angry with her until this afternoon. I'm sure I'll be exonerated soon."

"I hope so. I ran away from Jamie to investigate this crime scene."

"I'm sorry. I wasn't even thinking about your plans," Heather said. "I didn't mean to steal you away."

"It's not your fault. It's whoever-the-killer-is's fault. And he has other things to pay for besides ending my date early."

"That's true. How was furniture deciding?"

Amy groaned. "I'd rather track down a killer."

"That bad?"
"Neither of us want to give up certain pieces. And some things clash. And some things are heavy and are going to be impossible to move. The only thing I'm sure of is that the two of us will be inside the house. Everything else is debatable."

"Well, you two are the most important part," Heather said. "If you didn't take Jamie off the moving truck, it wouldn't be worth the move."

They started giggling as they formed the mental images of Jamie being unpacked from a moving box along with a plethora of packing peanuts. Ryan joined them, and they tried to quell their giggles.

"You're all cleared," Ryan said. "It looks like a bottle of wine was poisoned, and from what we've determined so far you'd have to have entered the house to lace it. Your movements are generally accounted for by witnesses today. You wouldn't have time to come here and kill her after she upset you."

"Glad to know you don't think I'm a killer," Heather said, smiling.

"Now let's see if we can find out who really did it."

"As if Heather could be a murderer," Amy muttered. "Though it would be our easiest case if all we have to do was arrest ourselves."

"The husband was home. He's the one who called the ambulance," Ryan said. "We have him in another room with Detective Hoskins right now, so I can show you the crime scene."

Amy and Heather exchanged a look.

"He's with Hoskins?" Amy asked.

"Do you think he's the most sensitive person to be dealing with the new widower?" Heather asked. "Isn't he more interested in food than witnesses?"

"You have to remember that the spouse is always a suspect," Ryan said. "And yes, he is still eating on the job, which in the case of a poisoning makes me nervous. We think it's only the wine bottle, but if it's somewhere else, I don't want my partner poisoned."

Heather nodded. Even if she thought Detective Hoskins was an ineffective partner for her husband, she didn't want him ingesting poison.

They followed Ryan into the spacious home and to the kitchen. It was a room that was generally tidy, but several items were knocked over. There was a round spot of liquid on the counter.

"Is that from the wine bottle?" Heather asked, pointing.

"Yes," Ryan said. "Forensics took it away already. Based on the smell and coloring, we believe there was arsenic inside, but they will officially confirm it with some more tests. They took the wine glass as well. That's what the red spill on the floor is over there."

"Why are so many things knocked over?" Amy asked. "Was someone trying to stage a break in as a cover for the murder?"

"I think it's from the death throes," Heather said. "As Marcia started realizing something was wrong, she sought help. Then her body started reacting to the poison, and she began flailing."

Amy shuddered, but then said, "Duh. I should have realized that."

"Any fingerprints?" Heather asked.

"Forensics took what they found to the lab. They'll have to compare them to the victim and the family first to determine if anything is helpful," said Ryan.

"If it was in the wine bottle, then it was intentionally put in?" Heather asked for confirmation. "There's no chance it was accidental."

"If it is both arsenic and in the wine bottle as we suspect, then it's definitely murder," Ryan said.

Heather frowned. She was not a fan of Marcia Lindau, but no one deserved to be poisoned. She would make sure that they caught whoever was behind this.

Chapter 7

"I can't believe this is happening," Dan Lindau said. He was holding his head in his hands as he sat on the couch opposite Detective Hoskins. "It was just like any other night."

"It's all right," Detective Hoskins said. "We'll get to the bottom of this. We're professionals." Then he offered Mr. Lindau one of his candies. "Would you like a toffee?"

"No. I'm not hungry," Dan Lindau replied.

"Suit yourself," Detective Hoskins said with a shrug.

Heather watched this scene and found it hard not to shake her head. Amy couldn't help herself.

"Come on," Ryan said.

The trio joined the detective and the spouse of the murdered woman in the living room. Ryan introduced Heather and Amy as private investigators who consulted on cases with the Hillside Police.

"We have to ask you some questions now," Ryan said.

"Go ahead," Dan Lindau said. "I want to find out what happened too. I just don't understand any of this."

"You were the one who called the ambulance?" Heather asked.

"Yes," he said. "I wasn't sure what was wrong, but it was obvious she needed help. I thought it was a heart attack or a stroke or something. But you think she was poisoned?"

"We're looking into that possibility," Heather said.

Amy took out their tablet so she could take notes during this interview. She opened the Evernote App and prepared to record what the spouse had to say.

"I don't know who would want to kill her," Mr. Lindau said.

"Your wife didn't have any enemies?" Asked Ryan.

"She wasn't perfect," Mr. Lindau said. "She might ruffle some feathers. But I can't think of any enemies. I can't think of who would want her to die."

"Whose feathers did she ruffle?" Heather asked.

"She could be pushy and particular. She was that way with everyone."

"Even you?" Heather asked.

"I loved her," Mr. Lindau said. "I think she might have ruffled some feathers at the PTA. I know not everyone wanted her to be president."

"Anyone in particular?" asked Heather.

"No," he said. "I can't always put names to faces in her stories. She has so many people that she talks about. The moms. The teachers. The kids. She expected me to know exactly who she was talking about all the time, so I just nodded and pretended a lot. Maybe that's a bad thing to admit now."

"I'm afraid we have to ask this," Heather said. "Were you and your wife having any troubles?"

"No, nothing. I admitted I wasn't perfect either because I couldn't keep up with all her gossip. But I would never kill her. And certainly not in a terrible way like this. When I was home, and I could see her suffer. It was terrible."

Detective Hoskins wanted to help, but all he could do was offer another toffee that Dan Lindau refused again.

"Can you take us through what happened tonight again?" Ryan asked.

"The only silver lining in all this," Mr. Lindau said. "Is that our daughter wasn't home tonight. She was at a sleepover so she didn't have to see what happened."

"Where is she staying?" Heather asked.

"With her friend Kiki Miller. Her mother and Marcia are friends. Were friends. Oh no, I have to tell them, don't I?"

"We can help inform whoever you need," Heather offered. "But first we need to ask you these questions because we need to find out what happened to your wife, and you're the one who can help us the most."

"Okay," Mr. Lindau said, trying to keep his cool in the height of great emotion. "The order of events. It seemed normal. I came home from work. I paid the babysitter and let her go home. Marcia came home from whatever event she was working on. We had a late dinner. Claire Miller and Kiki came to pick up Marlena for the sleepover. Then I watched some TV. I guess Marcia had a glass of wine. She does that most nights. And I guess that was what caused this."

"Do you ever drink wine with her?" Heather asked. She needed to determine if the killer killed the right person with their murderous drink. It was possible that the poison was meant for both parents.

"Sometimes," Mr. Lindau said. "I like beer better, but sometimes I'd have wine with her. Though I didn't really like red wine. I much prefer white."

Heather looked at Ryan.

"It was a bottle of red wine," he said to her. It looked as if the killer had laced the proper drink for only killing Marcia Lindau. If this was intentional, then the killer

81

knew the family's habits. If it was unintentional, then the killer was even more dangerous because he didn't care if anyone else got hurt as long as Marcia died too.

"I'd like to know more about that wine bottle," Heather said. "How long has it been in the house? Was it a gift?"

"I think it was one of the leftover bottles from Marcia's wine nights," Mr. Lindau said.

Heather nodded. She had heard a little bit about them at the bake sale. "This is where friends from the PTA come over for drinks?"

"It's a girls' night sort of thing."

"When was the last one?" Ryan asked.

"Just a few days ago," Mr. Lindau said. "On Friday."

"And who came?" Heather asked.

"Well, Claire Miller. And the tall brunette and the short brunette. And the one who always parks wrong in my driveway," he said. "I'm sorry. I'm not good with names."

"Did Marcia usually keep the wine bottles from these events?" asked Heather.

"Yeah. I think she kept the red wines. If it was unopened, she

83

might save it for the next meeting, but if it were open she'd keep it by her wine glasses and have some every so often. I guess she won't anymore."

Mr. Lindau looked like he was about to cry. Again, Detective Hoskins tried to help in the only way he knew how.

"Toffee?" He asked, offering again.

"No, thank you," Mr. Lindau said. "I'm diabetic and need to watch what I eat. Especially when I'm upset."

"You've been very helpful," Ryan said. "That's all our questions for now."

Heather and Amy thanked him as well, so did Detective Hoskins but his "thank you" was through a mouth full of candy.

"Now," Heather said. "What can we do to help with your daughter?"

Chapter 8

"Well, that was heartbreaking," Heather said, thinking about the night before and how they had helped Mr. Lindau explain to Marlena what had happened. They also notified Mr. Lindau's mother who was hurrying into town to care for her granddaughter while Dan Lindau dealt with his grief.

"Tell me about it," Amy said. They were enjoying a break at Donut Delights as they encountered a rare lull in between customers, but they were feeling anything but relaxed.

"We probably shouldn't get so involved when someone is still a suspect," Amy said. "But it's tough when kids are involved."

"I agree. But I think our help was all right as long as we continue to look at the case objectively."

"The spouse is always a suspect. It makes me want to never get married."

Heather gave her a look. She knew things were getting more serious between Amy and Jamie. Moving in together might only be the first step of many bigger ones. However, then Heather's thoughts drifted back to little Marlena.

"I don't ever want to leave Lilly alone like that. We have to make sure we don't get killed, all right?" Heather said, even though she knew making a promise like that was impossible to be sure of.

"I'm game if you are," Amy said. "Though we do get into some dangerous situations."

Heather thought about it. "Maybe I get into too many dangerous situations for a mom."

"What do you mean by that?"

"Well, investigating murders and chasing down killers is risky."

"So? What do you want to do?" Amy asked. "Do you want to retire?"

Heather wavered.

"Do you want to stop looking for Marcia Lindau's killer?" Amy asked.

"No," Heather said. "I know myself. I can't stop. Not when a killer is on the loose. Not when he thinks he can get away with murder. And not when he takes a mother away from a child."

"I don't want to stop either. So enough of this wishy-washy talk. Let's solve this thing!"

"Okay," Heather said, with a smile. "Let's discuss the case over some donuts."

Heather brought two donuts over to a table, and the friends sat down to eat and analyze.

"Any news from forensics?" Amy asked.

"Ryan did have some news for us," Heather agreed. "He confirmed what they thought about the wine. It was poisoned with arsenic. Though they think they were trace amounts of something else there too."

"Like what?"

Heather shrugged. "We'll have to wait and see."

"I hate waiting," Amy said.

"And the fingerprints news is a bust so far. They only fingerprints on the wine bottle were Marcia's."

"Poison is a tricky murder weapon," Amy said. "When a murderer kills with a knife, they obviously need to be with the victim at the time of death. But with poison, they can drop it in and walk away."

"Right," Heather agreed. "If Marcia had the wine bottle since her gathering on Friday, then there were many opportunities for someone to plant the poison."

"It could have happened at the party itself," Amy said. "As long as the killer was careful not to drink the wrong thing at the end of the night."

"Or the killer could have planted it when it was sitting on Marcia's counter any time during the last few days. That would mean that anyone who entered her house could have done it."

"So it was someone she knew well enough to invite inside her house," Amy thought aloud.

"Most likely," Heather agreed. "Though it is possible that someone could have sneaked inside without her knowledge."

They chewed on their donuts and their thoughts. There was still so much that they had to discover about the case.

"I feel like this is going to be a long list of suspects," Amy said. "Where do we get started?"

"We have to still consider Dan Lindau a suspect," Heather said. "He definitely had access to the wine."

"Right."

"And we should look into the ladies who went to the wine gathering."

"Short, tall, and bad parking job."

"That's them."

"I wonder what Tall's last name is?" Amy joked. "Could it be Drink-Of-Water?"

Heather laughed. "Dan Lindau might not know their names, but I'm sure they have them. There's a PTA meeting tonight that I think we should go to. If Claire Miller is the Claire I met at the bake sale, then I know who she is. And she could tell us who the other ladies are."

"One of them might have a motive for killing their friend."

"Or they might know of someone who has."

"Why are they having a PTA meeting tonight?" Amy asked.

"It was supposed to be about summer plans and how they would hit the ground running in the fall. Now it will probably be a bit of a memorial, and a bit of deciding who the new president will be," Heather said. "I bet we can get a lot of good information out of it."

"Then I'm happy to go with you," Amy said. "But if they serve any, I'm not having any of the wine."

Chapter 9

The PTA meeting was held in a school cafeteria. Heather and Amy arrived a little early and were surprised to see how many people were there as well. Perhaps parents were eager to find out how their children would be affected by a forced change in leadership, or perhaps morbid curiosity had brought people out of the woodwork to hear details about the murder. Regardless of the reason, Heather and Amy had to search out two seats together.

"This is more crowded than usual, right?" Amy asked.

Heather nodded. "I've only been to a few meetings, but it was never this full. It looks as if every parent is here tonight."

"Then there's a decent chance that the poisoner could be in this room," Amy said.

They surveyed the scene and tried to pick out the sad faces in the crowd.

"Do you think that's tall and short?" Amy asked, pointing to two brunettes who were dabbing their eyes with tissues.

Heather nodded. "They're next to the Claire I met, so they could be part of the wine crew."

They were soon joined by another woman wearing black who bumped into their table as she joined them. Heather and Amy nodded at each other. She was most likely the woman who Mr. Lindau deemed bad at parking.

Heather and Amy wanted to talk to them, but the meeting was beginning so they had to listen to old business and new business before they could begin interrogations. The meeting had a moment of silence for Marcia Lindau, and it was suggested that everyone who was able to should bring the widower a dish of food.

Claire was running the meeting as best she could, but often brought up how they would be searching for a new president and how anyone that wanted the job could submit their name for consideration. There didn't seem to be any takers at the moment. Many attendees wanted to hear details about the death, but Claire did her best to keep the meeting on track. It ended up being a short meeting because so many decisions were now up in the air. This meeting with a record attendance number couldn't have lasted more than twenty minutes.

However, the short meeting ended up working out for Heather and Amy. Instead of the attendees rushing off after a long meeting, eager to get home, they were dawdling and chatting.

Lisa from the scone table saw Heather and came up to her.

"It's crazy what happened, isn't it?" She said.

Heather nodded.

"I wasn't a fan of hers. And I think many people in this room had the same opinion." Lisa said. "But who would want to murder her?"

"We were wondering that ourselves," Heather said. "Do you have any suspicions?"

"I don't think I knew her well enough," Lisa said.

"You've never been to her house?"

"Nope," Lisa said. "I think I would have refused an invitation had I been invited. That seems very catty to admit now after her death. She did raise an awful lot of money for the school programs. I wonder who will take over now."

Heather shrugged. "Maybe one of her posse?"

"Maybe," Lisa said.

"Why don't we go ask them?" Amy said, providing an excuse for them to leave Lisa and go talk to the other ladies.

"Thanks," Heather said, as they made their way over to Marcia's friends. "I didn't want to be rude, but we do have to transition over into official business. I like Lisa, and it's reassuring to know that she hasn't been to the Lindau house."

"If she's telling the truth," Amy said. "If she broke into Marcia's house to poison her, she would hardly admit it."

"Spoilsport," Heather teased, but she knew that Amy was right.

They had to assume that anyone could be a suspect until the evidence told them otherwise.

She was eager to see if talking to Marcia's friends could lead them to some other suspects as well. They made their introductions. It was confirmed that Claire was Claire Miller, Kiki's mom.
Heather explained that they were private detectives working with the police to investigate Marcia's death and that they wanted to talk to them about the wine party.

"I don't believe it," Claire said. "They just want more gossip about her death like everybody else here. They just came up with a more convincing story to get more details about her."

"We really are working with the police," Heather said. "We have some I.D. and I can give you the number of the police station if you'd like to check."

Claire examined the I.D. badges that Heather and Amy showed her.

"I still don't know if we should talk to them," Claire said.

"Why not?" said the tall brunette whose name was Alexandra. "They're working with the police. Don't you want to know who killed Marcia?"

"Of course I do," Claire said. "I just want to make sure they're on the level."

"Perfectly on the level," Amy assured her. Then she unobtrusively pulled out the tablet to take notes on what the friends had to say.

"What do you want to know?" Alexandra asked.

"Were you all at the wine gathering on Friday? And was anyone else there?" Heather asked.

The women all nodded.

"We werc all there," Alexandra said. "And it was just us that night."

"Who provides the wine for these parties?" Heather asked.

"We normally all bring some bottles," Claire said.

"And because Marcia hosted, she got to keep whatever she wanted at the end of the night," Alexandra said. "She normally kept the reds."

"Were there any leftovers on this Friday?" asked Heather. She knew this was an important point to clarify.

"I think there was only one red left," Alexandra said.

The other ladies agreed with her. The woman who had trouble parking, whose name was Sally, agreed with gusto.

"I took the extra white wine home because I use it for cooking," Sally said. "There were two bottles. Marcia made a comment about how she did all the work for the party, but I was reaping all the benefits. I was leaving with two bottles of wine while she only had a half bottle."

Heather nodded. It might be impossible to determine exactly, but if they could determine how much wine was left in the bottle, it could help them figure out when the poison was put in the bottle. If she only drank it on the day of her death, then it could have been poisoned anytime between the wine party and when she drank. If she had a glass of wine in between, then the poison might have had to be inserted the day she was killed. Was the "half a bottle" description given from a group of friends that had been drinking enough to go on?

"Does anyone know her habits for drinking on days besides the wine gatherings?" Heather asked. The short brunette who was named Carmen shrugged. "I think most of us like a glass of wine here or there, but it also depends on the kids' schedules."

The women all nodded. Heather stopped herself from frowning in front of them. It was looking more and more difficult to narrow down the time frame for when the poison was put into the wine bottle. She would just have to establish whether anyone had a motive.

"Did you all get along with Marcia?"

"She was a great friend," Alexandra said.

"A real leader," offered Sally.

"A great planner," said Carmen.

"And the glue that held us together," said Claire.

"But," Alexandra said. "She could be tough on us."

"She could say cruel things," said Sally.

"Try to manipulate us," Carmen said.

"And undermine us at every turn," said Claire.

"But we're still devastated that she's gone," Alexandra assured them.

"Devastated," said Claire.

The other women all agreed. It seemed that Marcia could be difficult to get along with, even amongst her friends. But was this a reason to murder her?

"Did anyone visit Marcia's house this week?" Heather asked.

"I picked her daughter up for a sleepover the night she died," Claire said. "I didn't realize it would be the last time I saw her. I only went inside for a minute."

"I had to drop something off about a potential school trip," Alexandra said. "I went to her house for lunch the day before. The day before…"

"The night of," Heather asked, changing gears. "Did any of you notice anything strange about the red wine bottle that night?"

The women shook their heads. Heather thought it was too much to hope that they could offer her that piece of evidence where one of them saw another one pouring arsenic into the bottle.

"Was the bottle in the room and in everyone's sight the whole time?" Heather asked.

The women said that because they kept the red wine at room

temperature, it was kept in the living room where they met all night. They thought it was there in their sight the whole time, but couldn't be one hundred percent positive. It was possible that someone could have held a bottle when they went into the kitchen to grab a snack or new glass. It wasn't a behavior that would have stood out to any of them as peculiar. Also, no one there thought that their friend could be the killer.

"So who do you suspect killed her?" Heather asked.

"Well," Alexandra said. "I wouldn't normally give away her secrets, but if it might help catch her killer."

"We should tell," Claire said.

"Tell what?" Heather asked.

"Marcia was having an affair with one of the dads," Alexandra said.

"Spencer Port," said Claire.

"He and his wife were separated," Sally said. "And so Marcia started seeing him."

"We're not sure if Dan knew," said Carmen. "But if he knew, that could be a motive."

"Or maybe Mrs. Port got jealous," Claire said.

Heather thanked them for the information. Their suspect list had just gotten longer.

Chapter 10

When Heather and Amy arrived at Spencer Port's door the next day, they weren't sure what to expect of Marcia's alleged lover. However, the large balding man that they found was not on their list of expectations.

"Spencer Port?"

"Yes," the man said in deep soothing tones. "How can I help you?"

"I'm Heather Shepherd, and this is Amy Givens."

"How do you do?" He said with a voice as smooth as velvet.

"Fine, thank you. But we're private investigators, and we're working on a case with the Hillside Police. We're investigating the murder of a woman we believe you know. Marcia Lindau."

"Please come in," Spencer said, as he ushered them inside. He led them into the living room where there were some comfy seats and a piano. The walls were decorated with records and pictures of his son.

"When I heard she was murdered, I thought someone would want to talk to me."

"So you were having an affair?" Heather asked, deciding to be blunt and get a straight answer instead of dancing around it.

"Yes," Spencer said. "When my wife Susan and I separated, I felt like I wanted some company and to do something exciting. I am embarrassed to admit that my fling was with a married woman."
"How did this liaison start?" Amy asked, curiously. Spencer Port was not the usual lover that a woman like Marcia Lindau would take.

"She heard me perform. I'm an amateur opera singer, but not bad if I do say so myself. I seemed to impress her. She came up to me after a performance at a local theater. It started as asking if I might perform at a fundraising event, but it led to our becoming involved."

"Mr. Port, have you ever been to Marcia Lindau's house?" Heather asked.

"No, of course not," Spencer said. "She would come here for our dalliances."

"So you never went to her house?"

"We didn't want to run into her husband. She'd visit me here when my son was with his mother."

"And how would you describe your relationship with her?" Heather asked.

"What do you mean?" Spencer asked. "Do you want me to say it was illicit?"

"I mean, were the two of you getting along well? Or were there some issues?"

"Things were going just fine," Spencer said. "We both knew that this wouldn't last forever, but we didn't really think about that. We were having fun."

"We heard that she could be difficult to get along with," Amy said.

"We got along well. She liked to listen to me sing, and I loved to perform. That was one of the things that drove Susan crazy. She said I was too loud when I practiced. But when your voice is your instrument, you do need to exercise it."

"Was there anything else that drove Susan crazy?" Heather asked.

"Like what?"

"Like did she care that you were having an affair so soon to when you separated?"

"I think it might have irked her. But if you're suggesting that she killed Marcia, I couldn't believe it."

"I'm not suggesting anything," Heather said. "I'm just asking some questions."

"I think it did bother Susan that I was seeing someone else. I think Susan thought that we might reconcile, but she didn't want to work on fixing the problems that we had that led to our separation. If we didn't make any changes, we'd just be headed back to the same issues as before."

"But she did want you back?" Heather asked.

"Maybe she missed my serenades after they were gone," Spencer said, thinking about it.

Heather switched gears in her questioning. "Did Dan Lindau know about the affair?"

"I never met him so I couldn't say. But we were very careful. I don't think many people knew about us."

Heather and Amy exchanged a look. They had already encountered four people that had known about the affair. It was likely that more people knew about it too.

Heather thanked him for his time and was about to leave when he offered to sing them a song before they left. Amy couldn't resist hearing his voice and accepted immediately. Heather had never been serenaded by a suspect before but had to admit that he had a beautiful voice.

As they left his house and walked away together that was the first thing that she commented on to Amy. "He does have an impressive voice."

"I could see why Marcia was in to him," Amy said. "His talent is killer. But is he one?"

"I don't think so," Heather said. "He said he's never been to Marcia's house and that's where the killer would have to add the poison. He would be foolish to visit the house if Dan Lindau could catch him there. And because he's a larger fellow I think the neighbors might have noticed him breaking into the house if he attempted it."

"So he'd probably not the killer. But the affair could still be a motive. Marcia's husband or Spencer's wife could have been mad enough to poison her."

Heather nodded. "I think we have some more suspects to talk to."

Chapter 11

Susan Port had let them into her house but still wasn't very happy about talking to them.

"I don't understand why you're talking to me about Marcia Lindau's murder," she said. "I was never a member of the PTA, and the main reason was because of her. She was unpleasant, but I avoided her. I barely said two words to her."

Amy had pulled out the tablet and was taking notes to keep herself from saying anything too snarky.

"We believe you might have had a stronger motive for disliking her," Heather said.

"And why is that?" Susan asked. "Who told you that? Was it her little cronies? They were as bad as she was."

"You do seem to harbor some grudges against them all," Heather commented.

"No grudges," Susan said, in a voice of forced calmness. "I just didn't care for them. That's why I avoided them."

"There is a way to permanently avoid someone," Amy piped up.

"I didn't kill anyone," Susan said. "Did Spencer say I did?"

"Why do you equate a murder charge with your ex-husband?" Heather asked.

"He's still my husband," Susan said. "We may be separated, but we're not divorced yet. And our separation is actually pretty silly. I should never have recommended it. Spencer had been getting on my nerves with his constant practicing, and he said that I nagged all the time. But these are common couples' problems. We will overcome them."

"And yet you think that Spencer believes you murdered someone?" Heather asked.

"I didn't say that," Susan said. "I don't think."

"Is anyone else getting dizzy?" Amy asked. "I feel like we're running in circles."

"Fine," Susan said. "I know why you're asking me these questions. There's no more reason to beat around the bush. I know that Spencer was having an affair with Marcia."

"Finally," Amy muttered.

"And how did you feel about this?" Heather asked.

"How do you think I felt? Disgusted. They were both

cheating on the spouses," Susan said. "I was furious with Spencer."

"Were you furious with Marcia too?" Heather asked.

"I was angry at the time, but well," Susan said. "It seems like she's gotten her taste of karma, so I won't speak ill of the dead anymore."

Heather raised an eyebrow. That was an incredibly harsh thing to say. It seemed that Susan was emotional enough to have committed murder, but did she have the physical opportunity to commit the crime?

"Do you know where Marcia Lindau lives?" Heather asked.

"Why?" Susan responded. "Did someone say they saw me driving by her house? Maybe I drove by to see what that tramp was up to. But I didn't stop and sit there. For very long."

Amy made sure to take good notes during this interview. Susan Port was saying many incriminating things.

"You sat outside and watched her?" Heather asked.

"Just once," Susan said "But you have to understand I was very upset. I thought my husband and

I were going to reconcile and then I learned that this mean lady was trying to steal him from me. That she was trying to convince him that she was a decent human being. That's laughable."

"Mrs. Port, did you ever go inside Marcia Lindau's house?"

"Of course not," Susan said. "I'm not crazy."

Amy locked her jaw to keep her from saying something to rebut that statement.

"Did you ever get close to the house?" Heather prodded. "Maybe just to look in a window?"

"The closest I ever got was the street," Susan said. "I wasn't looking to fight the woman. And I certainly wasn't looking to kill her."

Heather thanked Susan Port for her time. She and Amy left quickly.

"Well, she jumped to the top of my suspect list," Amy said.

"She certainly showed that she had a motive," Heather agreed. "And if she were staking out the house, it would be possible for her to sneak inside after she learned the family's routine."

"Right," Amy nodded. "She could sneak inside, add the poison, and return to her car waiting on the street."

"She's definitely a strong suspect," Heather said. "But there's no smoking gun to tie her to the murder directly."

"Can you have a smoking poison?" Amy asked.

Chapter 12

"I knew we'd be coming back to talk to him," Ryan said. "But I didn't realize that we'd uncover an affair."

He stood on the doorstep to the Lindau house with Amy and Heather. They were all set to talk to Dan Lindau and discover what he knew about the affair.

Dan opened the door. He looked like he hadn't slept in days.

"This is good timing," he said. "My mother just took Marlena out for a bit, so we can talk about the death without upsetting them. Did you find out any more information?"

"We've found out some things," Heather said, evading an answer.

"We've learned the names of the people who attended your wife's wine gathering," Ryan said. "Maybe you could give us more details about them?"

"I'll certainly try," Dan said. "But I'm not good with names. And I didn't think any of her friends would want to kill her."

"Give it a try," Ryan said.

Dan agreed, and so Heather began listing names while Amy took notes.

"Alexandra Kerr."

"That name doesn't ring any bells," Dan Lindau said.
"She's the tall brunette," Heather said.

"Oh," Mr. Lindau said. "She seemed friendly. I thought she and my wife got along well."

"Sally Whitley."

"Who's that?" Mr. Lindau asked.

"The one who can't park," Amy said.

"She also got along well with my wife. They were all friends."

"What about Claire Miller? She was in the wine gathering too." Heather asked.

"That is a name and face I know because Kiki and Marlena are friends. Claire was probably Marcia's best friend too. No problems there."

"What about Susan Port?" Heather asked.

"I don't recognize that name," Dan said.

Then Heather asked, "How about Spencer Port?"

"Now what would a man be doing at the girls' wine night?" Dan demanded.

"How did you know Spencer Port was a man?" Ryan asked. "I know several women named Spencer."

"Unless you did know who Spencer Port was?" Heather prodded.

"You tricked me," Mr. Lindau said.

"We're trying to catch a murderer," Heather said. "We needed to know how much you knew."

"I didn't know," Mr. Lindau said. "At least not for sure, but I did suspect it. That my wife was having an affair."

"What made you suspicious?"

"The way she would answer her phone. And a few times she told me that she was going out with Claire, but then Claire wouldn't have any idea what I was talking about when I asked how the new restaurant they tried was."

"How did this make you feel?" Heather asked.

"More sad than anything," Dan Lindau said. "She was my wife, and I wanted to trust her, but she

141

was making it difficult. I thought about confronting her about it but was afraid of what she might say. What if I was wrong? Or what if she wanted to leave me for him when pressed? We had built a life together. And we had our daughter to think about."

"How a killer makes their kill says a lot about their state of mind. When someone stabs another person, they are usually filled with malevolent passion. They can act in the heat of the moment in anger. When someone poisons someone, it can take some time before the victim takes a sip. It can be a more calculated kill."

"I didn't kill my wife," Dan Lindau said. "I could never hurt her. And I wouldn't have left poison around the house. What if something went wrong? I live here too. I could have poisoned myself. Or what if something spilled and I had hurt my little girl?"

"You said you don't normally drink red wine. And your child wouldn't drink the wine either. It might have been a calculated risk," Heather said.

"No," Mr. Lindau said. "I didn't kill my wife. Even though she was having an affair, I didn't kill her."

The trio of investigators looked at one another.

"Thank you for your time today," Ryan said.

"We'll be in touch soon," said Heather.

Chapter 13

Heather was happy to take a little break from the case and enjoy a movie night with her family. She was feeling stumped by the case. There were so many opportunities for the killer to make his move, and there were so many suspects who could have done so. Luckily, she did know the answers to a happy movie night. It involved good friends, a fun film, and some donuts for snacks.

They decided to watch one of Lilly's favorite movies again, *Jurassic Park* and enjoyed some Funfetti Donuts as the dinosaurs moved about on screen. Dave and Cupcake were content to get donut scraps and have their fur petted. Eva and Leila enjoyed a lazy night in with friends after such an athletic night the other day. Amy had happily joined them for the movie but suggested that they watch her favorite *Beaches* next time.

Everyone was feeling lazy after the movie, and they just chatted together until they all became sleepy. Ryan arrived home from the police station just before it was time to put Lilly to bed. He and Heather kissed her goodnight, and then wished Eva and Leila a good night without the kiss.

They wandered into the kitchen where Amy had been waiting.

"I should be getting home soon, but I wanted to see if Ryan had any updates on the case."

"Nothing right now," Ryan said. "I was waiting for the new lab report to see if they determined what else was found in the wine. There were trace amounts of something else besides the arsenic."

"And they don't know what it is yet?" Heather asked.

"I asked Hoskins to send it to me if it arrived while I was out with you today. Then I was waiting for it this evening. I eventually got tired of waiting, so when I finished my other work I came home," he said.

"This is a tough case," Heather said. "Maybe whatever else is in that wine will give us the clue we need."

"That's why I've been so impatient for it," Ryan agreed.

"If the wine was out on her counter for several days there were many opportunities for the killer to tamper with it," Heather recapped. "A few people admitted to being in the house."

"Alexandra and Claire both said they were there," Amy said.

"And, of course, Mr. Lindau was in the house with access to the bottle," Ryan pointed out.

"And if anyone snuck into the house just to plant poison, they wouldn't admit to being in the house," Heather said. "There are just hours and hours where the wine could have been tampered with. And there are too many suspects."

"Is there anyone that jumps out at us?" Ryan asked.

"I hope not," Amy joked. "I don't want any killers jumping out at me."

They laughed and then thought about what Ryan was really asking.

"I think Susan Port is the most likely candidate," Amy said. "She tried to hide it at first, but it was clear she hated Marcia Lindau. And she might have thought that getting rid of her would help her get her husband back."

"She does have a strong motive," Heather agreed.

"And she knew where Marcia lived. She practically admitted to stalking her. She could have killed her as well," said Amy.

"Dan Lindau also has a strong motive, though he didn't appear as emotional when he spoke to us," Heather said.

"He had access to the wine all week," Ryan said. "He said that it would have been dangerous or him to leave the poison in his home, but he would have known what to avoid."

"I don't really think Spencer Port is the killer based on our meeting with him," Heather said. "But I'm not sure we can completely dismiss the lover."

"Then there are the friends from PTA," Amy said. "Marcia was difficult to get along with and might have pushed a friend too far."

"They'd certainly have an excuse to be there if they say they were visiting their friend," Heather said. "And two of them already admitted to visiting."

They all thought about it and then let out a collective groan.

"I'm just not sure how to narrow it down," Heather said.

Ryan's phone buzzed, and he read the message he was sent.

"This might help narrow it down," Ryan said.

"What is it?"

"The lab report about what else was in the wine."

"Why are you getting it at this time of night?" Amy asked.

"I don't want to think poorly of him, but I have a feeling that Hoskins was given this report earlier and forgot to give it to me."

Heather shook her head as she realized that was probably true. Could they have been without an important clue that could break the case for hours now? She couldn't wait any longer.

"What does it say?" she asked.

"Now this is interesting," Ryan said. "The trace amounts are insulin."

"Insulin?" Amy asked. "Why would that be in there?"

"Does it make the poison more potent or something like that?" Heather asked.

"I don't think so," Ryan said.

"Then why is it there?" Heather pondered.

They all thought about it. Finally, Amy said, "I just don't see what the purpose of it is."

"That's it," Heather said. "Or rather the opposite."

"The opposite of purpose?" Amy asked, trying to follow Heather's line of thought.

"Yes," Heather said. "If it's not on purpose, it's by accident. I bet the killer didn't mean to put the insulin in the wine. Why would they?"

"No idea," Amy said. "Is this their fatal slip up where we can catch them because of it?"

"I think that the killer inserted the poison into the wine bottle using a diabetic needle. One that used to hold insulin. The killer probably thought it was empty or clean, but there were still traces inside."

"If it was a wine bottle that was already open, did the killer need to use a needle to poison the wine?" Amy asked.

"Maybe. Maybe not," Heather said. "Depending on the circumstance of when it was poisoned, it might still have been ideal to go through the cork. Maybe it was faster. Or maybe the killer did remove the cork, squirt the poison in, and replace the top."

"But then why use the diabetic needle if that's the case? Amy asked.

"Because it's a lot easier to explain why you're carrying around a medical device than it is a vial of poison. This was actually pretty smart of the killer," Heather said.

"Smart?" Amy said.

"Don't worry," said Heather. "Not so smart that we can't catch him."

"Agreed," said Ryan. "And now who is someone on our suspect list that we already know if diabetic?"

Chapter 14

"Being diabetic doesn't make me a murderer," Dan Lindau said.

"Can you explain why insulin was found in the poisoned wine bottle?" Ryan asked.

"No," Dan said. "But I can't explain why there was arsenic in there either."

This time the interrogation was taking place at police headquarters. Dan Lindau was less collected when they last spoke as well. He seemed angry.

Ryan and Detective Hoskins were seated at the table across

from Mr. Lindau. Heather and Amy were relegated to a corner so that they would all fit inside. Heather didn't really mind. She thought Ryan was capable of "making the suspect talk" in this setting, and she was close by if there was an important question she thought of that needed to be asked.

Detective Hoskins was patting himself on the back for an entirely undeserved reason. "It was pretty smart of me to offer him those toffees," he said. "We found out he had diabetes and that seemed to be the break in the case. That was some good work I did."

Amy rolled her eyes.

"I didn't kill my wife," Mr. Lindau said. "And you're wasting your time talking to me instead of trying to find the person who actually did it."

"You can't pretend we're making up a case against you," Ryan said. "We know your wife was having an affair, which gives you a motive."

"But I didn't act on it. I was too afraid to confront her," Mr. Lindau said.

"You had access to the wine which served as the murder weapon for several days."

"I don't know what else you want me to say," Dan Lindau said. "I didn't do it."

"Traces of insulin were found in the wine, and you use insulin," Ryan continued.

"Maybe somebody is trying to frame me," Mr. Lindau said. "It's the only explanation I could come up with."

Heather thought of something else incriminating and piped up. "You were the one who called the ambulance. To an extent, you could control when they arrived."

"Are you saying I purposely made sure the ambulance would be too late to save my wife?" He asked angrily.

"It's a possibility," Heather shrugged.

"That thought already haunts me. If I had been just a little faster. If I had realized what was happening a little sooner. Could I have saved her?" Dan Lindau folded his arms. "I don't have anything else I want to say to you. I want a lawyer."

Ryan closed up his notebook and left the room with his cohorts, while Mr. Lindau waited for a lawyer.

"Well," Hoskins said, clapping his hands as if clearing dust. "Looks like this one is in the bag. Good work everyone. Even my toffees helped out. And to celebrate I think I might have some more."

Hoskins walked away, and Heather was pleased that the three hardworking investigators could discuss this turn of events more in-depth.

"I really thought he would confess," Ryan said.

"Something does seem a little off about this," Heather said. "Dan Lindau lived in the same house as Marcia. He probably wouldn't need a clever hiding place for his poison. He wouldn't have to carry it around in an insulin needle. He had plenty of time when he was alone in the house or others were sleeping to carry out this few second task."

"You don't think he did it?" Amy asked

"I'm just not sure," replied Heather.

"Is it possible he was right, and he is being framed?" asked Amy.

"It's possible," Heather said. "But it's a messy frame job."

"Why messy?"

"Well," Heather said. "We're lucky we have such a good forensics team that was able to analyze the tiny amounts of insulin in the wine."

"So if the killer was trying to frame Dan Lindau, he couldn't count on the insulin being found in the murder weapon?" Amy asked.

"I don't think so," said Heather. "And if someone really wanted to frame him, they could have squirted just as much insulin as arsenic into the wine. Why not?"

"That's true," Amy said.

"I'm not saying he definitely didn't do it. There are lots of things that point to him being guilty," Heather said. "It's just that there are some pieces to this puzzle that don't fit. And I hate it when the pieces don't fit."

Chapter 15

Feeling almost back to square one with suspects, Heather was happy to attend another PTA meeting. This one was more impromptu and had a much smaller audience. The aim of this meeting was to select an acting president until an official one could be put in place. Apparently, this drew a smaller crowd than the mystery surrounding Marcia Lindau's death.

Heather and Amy easily found seats this time and were joined by Lisa Luft.

"Are you going to run for president?" Lisa asked as she sat down.

"No," Heather said. "I have too much going on to give it my all."

"You seem like you might be good at it," she said.

"I'm not sure it's really my thing," Heather said. "I know what my real callings are, and I'm pretty happy with them, even though they do take up a lot of my time."

"What about you?" Lisa asked Amy.

"Oh, no," Amy said. "I barely belong in this room, let alone be the one to lead it. I'm neither a P nor a T. I'm just her friend, and we go everywhere together."

Lisa nodded along. "I wonder who they'll pick."

"What about you?" Heather asked the question back to her.

"Me?"

"I think you'd be a great president," Heather said. "You put people at ease rather than making them feel like they're in a competition that they are destined to lose."

"I never even considered it," Lisa said. "Do you really think I could do it?"

"Sure," Heather said. "And even at the bake sale, you were putting the consideration of the customers and children ahead of your own ego. I think this would be a welcome change."

"What if I can't raise as much money as Marcia could?"

"You'll never know unless you try," Heather said.

"You're right," Lisa said. "Sure. I'll try it."

With that she decisively went up to put her name in for consideration. Heather was very pleased when after a brief back and forth, Lisa was officially named as Acting President. Lisa didn't know that she would have to make a speech and literally had not prepared anything because she didn't decide to ask for the position until a few moments before the meeting.

However, Lisa said some nice things about how they could all work together to achieve some positive goals for the kids. She thanked Heather for encouraging her and looked excited to begin her new work.

Heather was happy that she was able to do some good work at the meeting before she even got to her questioning. She wasn't sure that she was going to uncover anything useful, but because she didn't have a "prime" suspect she thought she might as well talk to everyone again.

She and Amy walked up to Marcia's friends who were gathering together again.

"It's the investigators," Sally said.

"What do you think about that Lisa Luft as the new president?" Alexandra asked.

"I think she'll be fantastic," Heather assured her. "I think she really has a way with people and she's excited to do some new projects."

Alexandra smiled. "That's reassuring. We should go and welcome her to the position."

The other ladies agreed, but Heather held up a hand. "Before you go welcome her, we need to ask you some more questions."

"More questions?" Claire said. "You're going to make us think that you suspect us of the crime."

"No," Carmen said. "I heard they arrested Dan Lindau for the murder. Is that true?"

"He hasn't been arrested," Heather clarified. "He's just being questioned about what happened in a more official setting."

"So they don't think he did it?" Carmen asked.

"They're not sure right now," Heather said. "Do you think he could have done it?"

The ladies looked at one another.

"I wouldn't have thought so," Alexandra said. "But now that she has been murdered I'm not so sure."

"Somebody had to do it," Sally said.

"But do you really think Dan did it?" Carmen asked. "I feel like he doesn't have a fighting bone in his body."

"But maybe that's why he used poison," Claire said. "It has less direct contact, so maybe he felt brave enough to face that type of kill."

"He probably did know about the affair," Alexandra said. "Partners can usually tell."

"I just don't buy it," Carmen said. "He just doesn't seem like a murderer."

"Who does?" Claire asked.

"Is there anyone who could have wanted to frame Dan Lindau for the murder?" Heather asked.

"Frame him?" Sally asked. "Then you do think there is a lot of evidence against him."

"I can't believe a husband would kill his own wife," Carmen said.

"Why are you considering that he was framed?" Claire asked.

Heather and Amy exchanged a look. They didn't want to give too much information away about the case. They thought they should keep the insulin clue quiet for a while. Either the killer had thought that he committed a perfect crime and telling him about the insulin residue would alert him that he had made a mistake, or the killer actually had tried to frame Dan Lindau, and they didn't want him to know how seriously they were taking the clue.

"We're just considering all possibilities," Heather said. "Do you know anyone who had a grudge against Mr. Lindau?"

The ladies all shrugged and shook their heads.

"We didn't know him too well," Alexandra said.

"He was the significant other of a friend. Not our friend," Claire said.

"But he seemed well liked and got along with people," said Carmen.

"And Marcia didn't give us any gossip about his being involved in a feud," Sally added.

"I think she would have told us if he had any enemies," Alexandra agreed.

"She loved to gossip," Claire said.

"And to cause some drama," said Carmen.

"And talk about people being enemies," Sally said.
"Rest her soul," Alexandra said.
The friends all repeated after her.

"One last question," Heather said.
"Are any of you ladies diabetic?"

The shook their heads again.

"What a funny thing to ask?" Claire said.

"It must be about future bake sales, right?" Asked Alexandra.

Heather nodded along as they giggled and talked about how she balanced work and the PTA. Then they returned to their original idea of congratulating Lisa on becoming the acting president.

"If they swarm her every meeting, I'll start to think that my inspiring words to Lisa were actually a curse," Heather said.

"I think she'll survive," Amy said.

"I'm not sure we learned anything new from that conversation," Heather grumbled.

"Just that they don't know any reason why someone would want to frame Dan Lindau for his wife's murder."

"I really don't think he was framed," Heather said. "I just thought I should follow up on the idea for due diligence."

"Dan Lindau himself didn't offer up any ideas on who was framing him."

"I think that the insulin in the wine was a mistake," Heather said. "The thing that makes the most sense to me is that the killer carried the poison in a diabetic needle that they thought was empty. The trace amounts found in the wine bottle transferred accidentally."

"Dan Lindau could have still used the needle," Amy said.

"That's true," Heather said. "It needs to be someone with access to an insulin needle. I'm pretty sure you need a doctor's prescription for it, so that could limit who could have one easily."

"Right," Amy said. "And if the killer were just using the needle for transport, why would they lie, cheat and steal to get this type of needle? Especially if they thought it was empty. It must have been easy for them to get ahold of one."

"So the question is," Heather said. "Which of our suspects had access to the wine, the poison, and the needle?"

Chapter 16

"No, I'm not diabetic," Susan Port said. "And I'm not a murderer."

"I am sorry to bother you again, but we need to follow whatever leads we come across," Heather said.

"I guess I understand," Susan said. "You need to solve every murder, regardless of who the victim is."

"You know that when you say these things, it makes you sound guilty, right?" Amy asked.

"I will admit that I'm not sorry that she's gone, but I can't admit to anything else. I was never inside her house," Susan said. "I didn't poison her. Though I don't mind that somebody else took it upon themselves to do so."

"See?" Amy said. "You're doing it again. This makes you sound like you killed her."

"And you admitted to being outside her house before, following her."

"Yes. But I didn't go inside and murder her. Even though—"

"I'm going to stop you there," Amy said. "Three murder threats, even after the fact, is my limit."

***

That afternoon as Heather and Amy walked the pets with Lilly, they couldn't help but think about the case. Lilly had run a little bit ahead with Dave who wanted to investigate a particular tree and claim it as his own, so the two friends had a moment to talk about murder.

"Susan was certainly acting peculiar," Heather said.

"I'll say," agreed Amy. "Did she want us to think she was the killer?"

"I think if she were the killer, she wouldn't have acted so bold."

"Maybe she's a *bold* blooded killer," Amy joked.

Heather laughed. Then she shook her head.

"I'm having trouble making sense of this case," she said.

"Poison is tough to track," Amy said. "There were so many people who had the opportunity to lace the wine with arsenic."

"And a lot of people with a motive to," Heather agreed.

"I thought the insulin would have helped to simplify things, but the only suspect who is diabetic is Dan Lindau, right?"

"Right," Heather said. "Ryan did some checks to confirm it."

"But something about him committing the crime doesn't sit right with you?"

"Maybe I'm overthinking it," Heather said. "But I feel like if he were going to kill the person he lived with in a premeditated manner, he would have come up with a better plan."

"Not all killers are smart," Amy said.

"I know that. But something about Dan Lindau as the killer bothers me."

"He's the only diabetic suspect with a reason to kill Marcia. He has means, motive, and opportunity."

"I know, I know," Heather said.

"Is this not the only thing that's bothering you?" Amy asked.

Heather looked at her bestie. "You know me too well," she said.

"What is it? Cupcake didn't drag us through any mud on this walk today."

"It's Lilly," Heather said. "I'm feeling like I'm spending too much time away from her, trying to solve a case and I'm not even doing a stellar job on this one."

"We're doing fine," Amy said. "We're not finished yet. We'll catch the killer. If it wasn't Dan Lindau, then we just need to determine who else had easy access to the diabetic needles."

"Am I ignoring Lilly when I focus on criminals?"

Amy groaned. "Why don't you just talk to her? You might save yourself a lot of stress if you just ask her how she feels."

Amy took Cupcake's leash and led her to an interesting flower. Heather went over to her daughter.

"Dave is being really pushy today," Lilly teased. "And there's not even any donuts around."

"Dave, are you giving her trouble?" Heather asked. Dave looked sheepish for a moment and then wagged his tail.

Lilly looked at her mom. "Is everything all right, mom?"

"I wanted to see if everything was all right with you," Heather said.

"Why wouldn't it be?"

Heather shrugged. "I don't know. It was implied that I don't give you everything you need."

"Who said that?" Lilly asked. "Not me. I think you're the best."

"You don't mind that I'm running a business and being an investigator at the same time as being a mom?"

"I think it's amazing that you do all that," Lilly said. "Actually it makes you a great role model."

Heather felt that what her daughter was telling her was genuine and felt an immense weight lift off her shoulders. Where had all these doubts come from? Lilly was happy with her life and with her family.

"It makes me feel like I can do anything when I grow up," Lilly said.

Heather had to blink a few times to keep herself to from tearing up.

"You can do anything you want when you grow up," Heather said back to her.

"Plus," Lilly said, conspiratorially. "I'm a very lucky kid in other ways too. Besides having wonderful parents, I also get lots of delicious donuts."

Heather gave her a hug. "You're my daughter," she said aloud.

"And you're my mom," Lilly said simply.

Dave barked to join in the moment.

"Actually there is something that is bothering me a little bit," Lilly said, after thinking about it a bit. "But it's not you."

"What is it?"

"It's Marlena. She just lost her mom, and I think she needs a friend."

Heather was deeply touched. "Do you want me to set up a playdate with her?"

Lilly nodded. "But it doesn't have to be a playdate. It could be a talk date. Or just sit-with-someone-who-knows-what-you're-going-through date."

"I'll set something up as soon as I can," Heather promised. She knew that it might not be right away because Mr. Lindau was currently being accused of his wife's murder and might not be feeling too kindly toward the Shepherds.

Heather was just thinking about how proud she was of her daughter and about future playdates when a thought occurred to her.

"It's so simple," Heather said.

"What is?" Lilly asked. "Did you solved the case?"

"I might have," said Heather.

Lilly waved Amy over. "Come here," she called. "My mom just solved the case!"

Chapter 17

This time Heather was able to sit at the interrogation table with Ryan. Amy was seated in the corner, taking notes. Across the table was a disgruntled looking Claire Miller.

"I don't understand why I'm here," Claire said. "This investigator has been harassing me at PTA meetings about a murder, and now you're letting her convince you that I killed my friend."

"I should have realized how strange it was," Heather said. "The switch you made from the bake sale to the when we talked to you about Marcia Lindau's murder. I didn't appreciate its significance."

"What are you talking about?" Claire asked. "What switch?"

"At the bake sale when Marcia was saying I didn't give Lilly enough attention, you were the one who told her I was in the newspaper all the time for investigating crime."

"So?" Claire said, "Lots of people read the paper."

"Yes, but when Amy and I went to question you and your friends about Marcia's death, you said you didn't believe we were real investigators. You made us show you our identification."

"There's nothing wrong with being careful," Claire said. "There are a lot of imposters out there."

"It does seem strange to announce somebody as an investigator one day, and doubt their credentials the following day," Ryan admitted.
"So?" Claire said, "That doesn't prove anything."

"No, not by itself. You made a mistake, Claire," Heather said.

"What do you mean?"

"There were traces of insulin in the wine bottle," Heather told her.

Claire paled but pretended not to understand the significance. "I don't know what you're talking about."

"I realized that the killer must have carried the arsenic in a diabetic insulin needle and then inserted it into the wine. It was a convenient carrying case for them, and they would have an excuse for having a large needle with them if they were caught with it by saying it was a medical device."

"I still don't see what this has to do with me," Claire said quietly.

"We made a mistake in our thinking though," Heather said. "We kept assuming that it was the killer who had diabetes. But the killer didn't have to be. She could have gotten the needles another way."

"I didn't rob any medical supply stores recently," Claire said bitterly.

"You didn't have to," Heather said. "Your daughter has diabetes. You could have just taken one of her used needles. You thought it was empty and could be used to carry the poison into Marcia's house."

"Just because my child has diabetes doesn't make me a murderer."

"That's true," Heather said. "But you also had the opportunity to plant the poison."

"Any of the girls at wine night could have poisoned her," Claire said.

"But it didn't happen at wine night," Heather said. "You put the poison in the bottle when you picked Marlena up for the sleepover."

"You could easily have gone into the kitchen for a moment while waiting for the girls to get ready and committed the deed," Ryan said.

"It was the only kindness in a horrific act," Heather said. "You wanted to make sure the little girl wasn't home when you murdered her mother."

"This is all circumstantial," Claire said. "You don't have any proof."

"We're working on it," Heather said. "They found the trace amount of insulin in the wine. I'm sure the talented forensic lab workers can find out more specifics about it. Every batch is slightly different. They can track what went to your daughter and compare it to what killed Marcia."

Claire couldn't tell if she was bluffing or not. She started to look like a caged animal. Her eyes darted around the room.

"But wasn't she your friend?" Heather asked. "Why did you kill her?"

"My friend," Claire said aloud.

"I only saw a little bit of the interactions between you both. She was belittling you and telling you to be quiet. Quiet, Claire," Heather said.

Claire started to take deep breaths. She was getting upset.

"Of course, maybe you liked it when she was mean to you in front of others."

Claire gritted her teeth.

"Maybe you liked being told to be silent. Quiet, Claire."

"No!" Claire finally shouted. "I don't want to be quiet. I hated when she told me to be quiet. She was a terribly mean woman, and I hated her. She wasn't a friend. She was a queen who lorded power over us peons, and she deserved what she got."

"What did she deserve?" Heather asked quietly.

"She deserved to choke to death. So she would finally be the quiet one."

"You killed her?" Ryan asked.

"Yes. I killed her," Claire said. "And I'd do it again too."

"Claire Miller," Ryan said. "I'm going to have to arrest you for the murder of Marcia Lindau."

"Good," Claire said. "I want everyone to know it was me. I finally silenced her."

Chapter 18

Heather put the finishing touches on her Funfetti Donut tower and started into the backyard to deliver them for the girls to enjoy. Kiki and Marlena were both going through a rough time, but Lilly wanted to do what she could to help them get through it. It was a somber playdate, but Heather was glad she had arranged it.

"I know it feels really terrible right now," Lilly said. "I went through something similar. And I just want you to know it can get better."

"I don't see how," Marlena said. "My mom is gone forever."

"And you'll miss her forever," Lilly said, showing wisdom beyond her years. "But you can miss her and still have friends too."

"My mom ended up being a bad lady," Kiki said. She was both sad and embarrassed.

"My other dad was too," Lilly said.

"How do you deal with it?" Kiki asked. "I want to go screaming into the woods and hide and never come out."

"I guess I found people that I really care about and some hobbies that make me feel special and I latched onto them."

"I guess I could latch onto my dad," Kiki said. "He was really upset by all this too. He said my mom had always been so quiet."

"I just feel sad," Marlena said.
"It's okay to be sad," Lilly said. "But it's okay to feel other things sometimes too. It's okay to be a little happy when something good happens even when you're overall still really sad. I found that donuts are great with that."

Heather took that as her cue and delivered the donuts to the girls. A small smile did come to each of their faces as they ate something yummy.

"We can just sit and talk for a while if you want," Lilly said. "Or we could play a game if you'd rather do that."

"Maybe we can just sit for a little bit," Marlena said. "And maybe later we'll try a game."

Lilly nodded. "That sounds fine."

Heather went inside, feeling like a proud mama.

"What are you so happy about?" Amy asked.

"I love the person that Lilly is growing up to be," Heather said simply.

"Well, she did have a good role model," said Amy.

"I can't take all the credit," Heather said. "She's wonderful on her own."

Eva and Leila popped their heads into the room.

"We heard a rumor that there was a tower of donuts," Eva said.

"I wouldn't mind being locked up in one of those," said Leila.
"There was one, but I delivered it to some little girls who needed a pick-me-up."

Eva and Leila nodded, trying not to look crestfallen.

"However," Heather said. "I do have more Funfetti Donuts lying around if you're interested."

"Of course we are," Eva said.

"Are you kidding?" asked Leila.

Heather chuckled and brought out one of her secret stashes of donuts. They bit into them and enjoyed them just as much as when they first taste tested them.

"So colorful, and so enjoyable," Leila said.

"And we'll be needing the energy these doughy desserts provide us," Eva said. "We're off to play Pickleball again."

"Again?" Heather asked. "You two are on your way to becoming professionals."

"Well, we might join the Pickleball club and play more regularly," Eva confessed. "It was fun being a little competitive."

"It's fun for us because we were pretty good at it," Leila said with a laugh.

"Let me know about any upcoming games," Heather said. "I'm intrigued, and I've love to come to one."
"And if you two continue to build strong muscles from this game, I'll have to recruit you to help me and Jamie move."

"Oh, look at the time," Leila said.

"We've got to run," Eva agreed.

They took a donut for the road and speedily headed out. Heather and Amy laughed. Ryan entered the room.

"What was all that commotion?" Ryan asked.

"My friends are already trying to bail on helping me move," Amy said.

"How are your move in plans going?" Ryan asked.

"We settled on a couch," Amy said. Ryan didn't look duly

impressed, so Amy continued, "That was a huge deal."

"I believe you," Ryan said with a smile. "But after solving that case, I think anything else would seem easy."

"This was a tough one," Heather admitted. "If we didn't get Claire to confess, I'm not sure what we discovered would have held up in court."

"The lab techs couldn't really determine that the insulin came from a specific user?" Amy asked.

"I didn't think that was possible," Ryan said.

"It sounded impressive though," Amy admitted.

"I had a feeling that Claire Miller wanted to confess and talk about what she had done after being downtrodden by Marcia Lindau for so long. I'm glad we were able to get her talking," Heather said.

"You were great with the interrogation," Ryan complimented her.

"Thanks," Heather said. "But we should probably stop talking about Claire while her daughter is here. I don't want to upset her."

"How is this playdate going?" Ryan asked. He had been wary about the idea of bringing the victim's and the killer's daughters together, even if they had been best friends before the ordeal. He also wasn't sure that he wanted Lilly to be involved in the potential drama.

"As good as gold," Heather said. "I think having Lilly as a friend is exactly what they need right now, and Lilly is happy to help her new friends."

The peeked out the window and saw that the girls had decided to play a game. It was low-key but made Heather think that everything was going to be all right.

"You have a huge smile on your face," Ryan commented.

"I was just thinking," Heather said.

"About what?" He asked.

"How glad I am to have a little girl."

"Me too," he said, giving her a hug.

"Don't get too mushy," Amy chided. "I am still standing right here."

The parents kept hugging but laughed as they did so. Amy joined them at the window, and they watched the girls play their sweet game. It was a peaceful moment, and Heather felt truly calm.

"Oh, I forgot to tell you," Ryan said.

"What?"

"I ran into the new PTA president, Lisa. She said she was a friend of yours."

Heather nodded. "I like her a lot."

"Well, she wanted to know if you could bake a couple of hundred donuts for another bake sale. She seems really gung-ho on making money for the club."

Heather felt her calmness start to ebb away, but all she could do was laugh.

The End

A letter from the Author

To each and every one of my Amazing readers: *I hope you enjoyed this story as much as I enjoyed writing it. Let me know what you think by leaving a review!*

I'll be releasing another installment in two weeks so to stay in the loop (and to get free books and other fancy stuff) Join my Book club.

Stay Curious,
Susan Gillard

Made in the USA
Middletown, DE
15 August 2017